O9-BUB-523

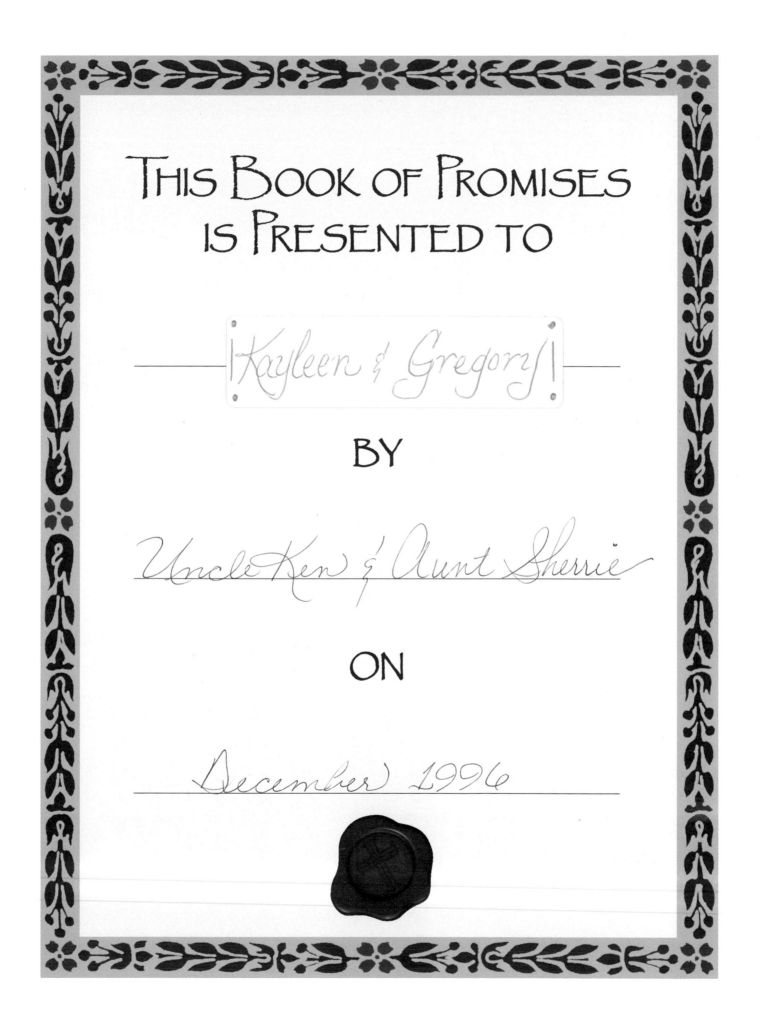

THIS BOOK OF PROMISES IS PRESENTED TO

Kayleen & Gregory

BY

Uncle Ken & Aunt Sherrie

ON

December 1996

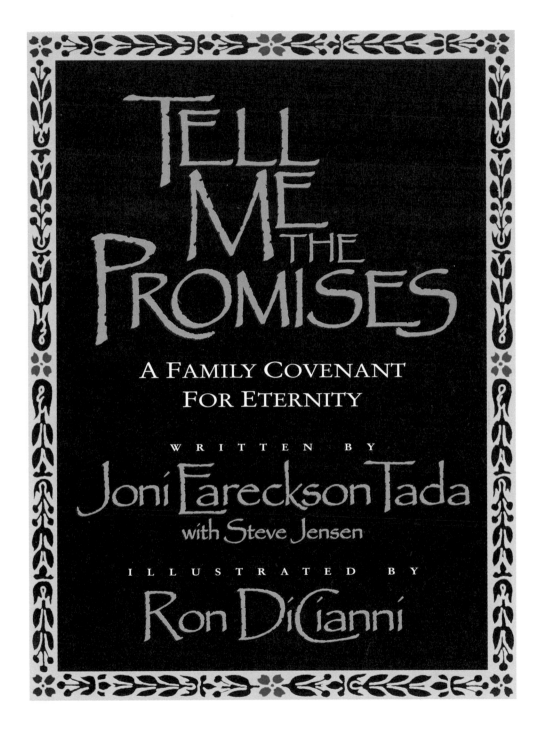

TELL ME THE PROMISES

A FAMILY COVENANT FOR ETERNITY

WRITTEN BY

Joni Eareckson Tada

with Steve Jensen

ILLUSTRATED BY

Ron DiCianni

CROSSWAY BOOKS • WHEATON, ILLINOIS

A DIVISION OF GOOD NEWS PUBLISHERS

FROM THE AUTHOR

To Margie and Carroll . . .
of such is the kingdom of heaven.

FROM THE ARTIST

To my sons, Grant and Warren,
my two greatest works of art to whom I have
the privilege of making promises

Tell Me the Promises

Copyright © 1996 by Joni Eareckson Tada

Published by Crossway Books, a division of Good News Publishers
1300 Crescent Street, Wheaton, Illinois 60187

All rights reserved. No part of this publication may be reproduced, stored in a retrieval system or transmitted in any form by any means, electronic, mechanical, photocopy, recording, or otherwise, without the prior permission of the publisher, except as provided by USA copyright law.

Illustrations: Ron DiCianni

Art Direction/Design: Cindy Kiple

Cover illustration: Keith Stubblefield

First printing 1996

Printed in the United States of America

Scripture is taken from the *Contemporary English Version of the Bible*.
Copyright © 1991, 1995 American Bible Society. Used by permission.

Library of Congress Cataloging-in-Publication Data
Tada, Joni Eareckson.
  Tell me the promises / written by Joni Eareckson Tada with Steve Jensen ; illustrated by Ron DiCianni.
      p.   cm.
  Summary: A collection of seven stories written to illustrate commitments between parent and child such as always protecting the child and always telling the truth.
  1. Children's stories, American. [1. Promises—Fiction. stories.]
I. Jensen, Steve. II. DiCianni, Ron, ill. III. Title.
PZ7.T116Te 1996   [Fic]—dc20   96-15688
ISBN 0-89107-904-1

04		03		02		01		00		99		98		97		96
15	14	13	12	11	10	9	8	7	6	5	4	3	2	1

Special Thanks

It was a hot September afternoon. I watched from under a shade tree as some friends worked with a local Boy Scout troop to load wheelchairs in a cargo container headed for Guatemala. One boy stayed on the fringe of the action. Ten-year-old Pete was a tagalong, a neighbor of one of the scouts. He was sweaty and tired, and so with a soda in hand, he plopped down next to me under the tree. After we talked awhile, Pete told me he had been suspended from school. His brother was a gang member. Pete didn't know where his mother was. His father was a recovering drug user.

My heart bled for this little guy, and so I spent the next half hour telling him my story—how I, too, had once done something "really stupid" by ignoring the rules and diving into shallow water. He leaned on his chin and became fully absorbed in my journey through hospitals, depression, and finally to the place where I could now sit before him and smile. All because of Jesus.

As we talked, I thought, *Oh, how I wish I had a storybook I could read to this boy. He's thirsty for the Lord Jesus, and he doesn't know it!* The next week my friends from Crossway called about the possibility of writing this book for children. Immediately I thought of Pete and thousands like him. And so I thank Pete.

And I thank Robert Wolgemuth of Wolgemuth and Hyatt for connecting me with my new friends at Crossway. My deepest gratitude to Lane Dennis, Len Goss, Lila Bishop, and others at Crossway Books for spearheading the idea for this book and following through with good taste and great enthusiasm.

Finally, as one artist to another, I thank you, Ron DiCianni, for your commitment to excellence. Your joy and creative drive helped make *Tell Me the Promises* happen—and happen in the best way. Keep painting for His pleasure!

—Joni Eareckson Tada

Thanks to my wife, Pat, who was the first to recognize God's will for me when we were just kids.

To Joni. Thanks for your obedience.

To my Crossway family. You are great partners.

To my heavenly Father. You gave me this project and the help and strength to complete it. Like a child, I put a bow on it and give it back to You, as though it were my gift. Somehow I know that makes You smile.

—Ron DiCianni

A Word from the Artist

In the Fire

It's unavoidable, isn't it? Being in the fire, I mean. It happens to all of us regardless of status, color, or age. Sooner or later we find ourselves in a situation that is out of control. *Our* control, that is.

One thing we know from Scripture is that no situation is ever beyond God's control. One day I am looking forward to asking the three brave Hebrews who faced King Nebuchadnezzar's fiery furnace how it felt when they realized they were not in that fire alone. And we are not alone in our fiery trials either. The "fourth Man" stands in the furnace with us to keep us from being destroyed—because we are precious to Him. What confidence that should give us—and our children.

Angels Unseen

The power of a parent's prayer cannot be overestimated. I've heard countless stories of these prayers and their answers. Sometimes the situation seemed impossible, but God honored those moments when a parent stood before His throne begging for His intervention. He answers in His own time and in His own way. Not one prayer goes unheard.

We do well to start the process of praying for our children early—while they are still in the womb even. We commit them and their futures to God before the events happen. For years I've been praying for the mates God will provide for my boys. Before they could walk, I prayed that God would use them to His glory in their future careers.

This painting depicts one result of prayer—as promised in Scripture (Psalm 34:7). Someday we'll know what dangers we escaped through the help of God's angels. That comforts me when I'm waiting for my sons to drive home.

Always

I'm well aware of the changing stages of life. I now have a son who is driving. Need I say more? However, I seem locked in to thinking of my boys as "little ones." No matter how big they grow, I will always remember holding my infant sons in my arms and singing them to sleep. The boys grow and mature, but some aspects of our relationship never change.

Our heavenly Father is even more consistent in His relationship to us. He never changes. Our mistakes don't phase Him. Our immaturity never causes Him to give up on us. To Him we are forever a delight. Every morning. Hard to believe He loves what I see in the mirror when I get up. He always sees the person I was created to be.

Maybe we can't slow down the march of time, but as in the image in the mirror of the painting, we can choose to see our kids through eyes of love. We can see the person God created our child to be.

The Prodigal

I'll bet he never intended it. As a boy, he probably was a good kid, a joy to his parents. I wonder what happened? Most likely the same thing that happens today. City lights look brighter when you're told not to go there. Dangerous companions suddenly seem irresistible. It's a story repeated a thousand times a day. And a thousand times a day Satan laughs. Another sale. Another promise of incredible pleasure. But watch the return on this investment. What? The pleasures didn't last? They never do. The scars might, but not the excitement.

Whatever you choose, remember this: *U-turns are okay with God.* And, oh, yes, He'll still have your robe and slippers waiting. God never turns out the night light. Hey, He gave you parents, didn't He?

Heavenly Help

My paintings usually don't need much explanation, but this one may be an exception. If you get the idea that the father here is saving his daughter from going over the side of the cliff, you're mistaken. As she attempts to make her way down a tricky ledge, symbolic of life, Dad sees an opportunity to help. Pure and simple. The hand to steady her, just in case, is not given *after* she stumbles—but to keep her from stumbling. Sometimes a parent has x-ray vision—the ability to see trouble ahead, though the kids don't see it coming. How like our heavenly Father! "So do not fear, for I am with you; . . . I will strengthen you and help you; I will uphold you with my righteous right hand" (Isaiah 41:10).

TRUTH

A banner hanging in Castle Hemingham in England reads: "Nothing is truer than truth." No matter how sincere someone is, if what he believes is not the truth, he is deceived.

Who decides what truth is? Pure and simple, truth is God's Word. In the Bible are His own words so that there would be no mistake. While it may seem possible today to create truth—if you can gather enough people in sympathy with your cause—the day is coming for a final accounting of what is true and what is false. No lawyers will present their case. No picket lines will protest the rulings. Only two classes of people will be present—those who lived by God's Word and those who didn't. And when the sentences are handed down to those who didn't, there will be no plea bargains.

We are fortunate to be able to deliver the absolute truth of life to our children. They should not be at the mercy of teachers, friends, or the media in looking for truth. Not when we have it setting on our coffee tables.

HEAVEN'S DOOR

On October 1, 1971, I came home to an empty house. That was unusual, but I figured that my mom had gone shopping. Until I saw the note. She had gone to the hospital to be with my dad who had had a heart attack at work. He died before she got there.

My last memories of Dad are good ones. Only a week before he died, we were hugging and affirming our love for each other. Sometimes I wonder if he can look down from heaven and see me. Does he rejoice at what the Lord is doing with his kid? Is he proud? Sometimes I ask the Lord to relay my love to him—if He sees him that day.

God's Word assures me that we will be reunited someday (John 14:2). For that to happen, I must go through a doorway, but I'm ready for that door because I have accepted Christ as Savior.

In this painting the shadows on the door represent the uncertainties we face on this side of heaven. The dark colors contrast with the magical colors on the other side of the door. A magical kingdom—prepared just for us.

A WORD FROM THE AUTHOR

Ask any boy or girl, and you'll hear it from the heart: promises are made to be kept. And there's nothing more precious than heartfelt promises forged between a parent and a child, whether it's a promise to get tickets for a baseball game, attend a school play, or read a story at bedtime. A child knows that commitments count. However, certain promises are more important than others—milestone promises about prayer and protection, forgiveness and love.

Kids today are thirsty for promises like that. That's because kids today live on a planet where people rarely can depend on each other to live by their word. It's a disposable world out there, and lots of things get tossed aside, including a person's pledge. Little wonder that the future is full of fear for so many children. But when a parent makes a promise—and determines to stick by it—a child's trust and confidence build. Confidence not only in the adult, but in God.

This is why I've written *Tell Me the Promises*. Yes, my friend Steve Jensen and I have written a series of stories that tell about "being there" or "lending a listening ear," but it's more than that. Each story is a direct invitation to strengthen precious commitments between you and the child whom you love. And after each story, you can seal it. Literally. I've even given you the proverbial "dotted" line.

So enjoy. Don't rush through. Take time to talk about these seven promises that will bind your heart to your child's. And linger long together over the powerful paintings Ron DiCianni has created to illustrate each commitment. When words and images blend, as they do in this book, then each milestone promise is magnified. Ron and I planned it that way.

After all, you hold in your hands what will become a family treasure, a keepsake record of seven key promises you will make to your child. I've written some stories from the point of view of angels. Others take place at playgrounds and picnic tables. Whatever the scene, the theme is the same. Each story relays a timeless promise.

A promise to be made . . . and kept.

IN THE FIRE

I PROMISE I WILL ALWAYS PROTECT YOU

We know that God is always at work for the good of everyone who loves him. They are the ones God has chosen for his purpose, and he has always known who his chosen ones would be. He had decided to let them become like his own Son, so that his Son might be the first of many children.

ROMANS 8:28-29

There once was a city of fantastic splendor. Tall buildings, beautiful art, and great riches could be found there. But though its splendor was great, the city was evil. Its rulers acted like criminals, and its citizens lived in fear.

Unlike the rulers of the city, the king of the realm to which the city belonged was wise and patient. He had granted the city time to change its ways, but year after year the city's sin grew greater. One day the king's patience came to an end. "It is time," he said to his court. "I will appoint a new ruler for the city, one who will govern as I would."

The king turned to his messenger. "Go into the countryside. The first man you see working in the fields before the sun has risen is to be brought to me. Bring him through the city as you return."

The messenger did as he was commanded. One cold morning after several days of riding, and just before sunrise, he saw a man working in a field. He called out, "Hail, farmer! I have come from the king!"

"What does my king want?" the farmer answered the approaching messenger.

"He has need of you."

"And his purpose?"

"He will tell you when you arrive. He gives you this letter to carry for your protection," the messenger said as he handed the farmer a letter.

The farmer opened it and read:

The bearer of this letter is under my protection. Treat him as you would my son.
This is my seal,
The King

7

The farmer folded the letter and at once began to walk. "Are you coming with me or not?" he asked the messenger. "I will not keep His Majesty waiting."

Within a few days, the farmer and the messenger arrived at the west gate of the city.

"Take care as we proceed, farmer," the messenger said. "If we keep to ourselves, we will be safe."

It was good advice but not obeyed. For immediately after entering the city, they heard a scream. The farmer turned to run toward the cry.

"Stop!" the messenger said, gripping the farmer's arm. "It is not our mission to heed such cries."

But the farmer broke free and answered sharply, "Any mission for a kind king could not do otherwise! Let's go!"

The messenger followed the farmer to an alley where they saw a woman huddled in a corner. The farmer bent down to comfort her but was immediately surrounded by three hooded figures waving knives.

"Welcome to our trap!" one of them sneered. "And good show, my lady," he added, speaking to the woman. She stood and joined the attackers.

"Let this be a lesson to you," the woman mocked. "Don't meddle in other people's business. Now give us your money!"

"As you wish," the farmer said, "but you should know that we are under the king's protection. Here is his letter—"

The thieves broke into loud laughter.

"The king? A letter of protection? Be serious, farmer! Your letter means nothing to us!" With that the woman grabbed the farmer's money and ran away with her partners.

The two travelers stared after the disappearing thieves.

"Will you listen now to my advice?" asked the messenger.

"We will see, my friend," answered the farmer. "I make no promises but to obey my king."

Making their way to the center of the city, the two men soon came upon a horrible sight. In the park, a crowd had gathered around a man and a boy. The boy knelt on the ground, covering his head with his hands. The man stood above him with a whip, laughing as he brought it down on the boy's bare back.

"I already know what you want to do," the messenger whispered to the farmer. "You have a heart to meddle, do you not?"

The farmer left the messenger without reply, broke through the crowd, and placed himself between the man and the boy. "Stop! What is the meaning of this cruelty?"

"Meaning?" the man asked. "There is no meaning except that this boy is a thief, and I am the sheriff. And you are in my way!"

"But has this boy had a trial?" the farmer asked boldly.

"Trial?" the sheriff laughed. "Obviously you are a stranger here."

"That is true, Sheriff. But the king's justice is not served without a trial."

"And who are you to challenge *my* justice?"

"A man on a mission for the king."

"Then you shall finish your mission in my jail!" The sheriff grabbed the farmer and began to drag him away.

"But I am under the king's protection! Here is his letter!" The farmer pulled it from his coat.

"This letter is worthless!" laughed the sheriff as he read it. "My jail can offer better protection!"

The farmer was led away to spend the night in jail. He lay awake until early the next day when the sheriff threw him out into the street. The awaiting messenger greeted him.

"Are you finally ready to continue without stopping for others on the way?" he asked.

The farmer shook his head. "Kindness and justice are costly in this city, I grant you. But such a promise cannot be kept. Not while I seek the king."

The travelers could see the king's castle in the distance as they left the city through the east gate. There they approached two men in the road, arguing loudly and waving clubs above their heads.

The messenger spoke first. "I am afraid to ask, farmer, but will you seek peace between these men?"

The farmer paused. The attack of the thieves followed by the night in jail tempted him to give up his love for people. And he had even begun to doubt the king's ability to protect him. But he knew no other course than that which his heart had set.

"It is as you fear, messenger. But what else can I do?"

He led the way and approached the shouting pair. "Stop, men! Settle this quarrel now before blood is shed!" He placed a hand on each man's shoulder.

"And whose side are you on?" one of them asked angrily.

"I am on the side of the king. And I seek only what he seeks in this matter—peace. Please lay down your weapons."

The pair smiled at each other upon hearing the farmer. "Seems a fool has stumbled into our fight, brother," one said. "What say we stop long enough to get rid of him and his slave."

The messenger stepped forward to protest, but the farmer held him back.

"The king has given us his protection." The farmer held out the letter for the pair to read.

Evil grins broke across their faces. "He has a letter from the king, brother! And it says we should treat him like the king's son. Shall we?" Whereupon the brothers attacked the travelers, beating them cruelly and laughing as they did so.

The beating stopped when the attackers got bored and left the pair to die. It was not until late in the day that a member of the king's court happened upon the injured men and brought them back to the castle. The messenger was near death, the farmer badly hurt but strong enough to move about.

"I must see the king," he moaned in pain.

The farmer's wish was granted. As he was led to the court, he vowed to withhold his anger at the way he was treated on his journey. But upon seeing the king comfortably seated on his throne, the memory of the journey was too much to bear.

"I left my peaceful home to obey your command!" he accused the king. "And I traveled at great peril! I have been robbed, jailed, and beaten! The citizens of the city, of your kingdom, are monsters! And worse still, your letter of protection meant nothing! Why? Why?"

The room was silent for several moments as the king gazed at the injured farmer.

"Welcome," he said at last, seeming to ignore the man's anger. "I have been waiting for you. You are, as I thought, the man I need."

"For—for what, Your Majesty?" the farmer stuttered, confused by the king's greeting.

"Why, to rule the city, of course. You are a man of kindness and justice and peace. This is what the city needs in a ruler. Do you not agree?"

"Yes, but . . ." The farmer paused in disbelief. He was still hurt and confused by all that had happened. "Your letter—why was I not protected?"

"Come," the king commanded. "I will show you." He led the farmer to a mirror beside the throne. "Do you see our images there?" he asked.

"Yes."

"And what do you see?"

The farmer laughed softly. "I see a poor farmer clothed in rags, with cuts and bruises, standing next to a king in royal robes."

"True, farmer. But look again. This time look into your eyes. There you will see what was protected. For it was not your body that needed protection, but rather your heart, because you have been chosen to be my heir. My subjects' evil actions toward you, born of their hatred for me, have refined and shaped you as a man. It had to be so, for you were meant to reign in my image."

The farmer gazed intently into the mirror. As he did so, his ragged clothes, his wounds, his bruised body all faded from view. What he saw was the man he had become—a man whose character could stand against the fires of evil. He had known the king's protection after all. He knelt on grateful knees before the king.

"Come, my son," the king said as he laid his hands on the farmer's head. "Your reign as prince has begun."

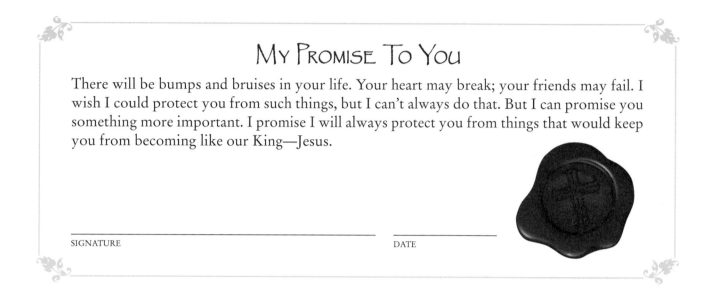

My Promise To You

There will be bumps and bruises in your life. Your heart may break; your friends may fail. I wish I could protect you from such things, but I can't always do that. But I can promise you something more important. I promise I will always protect you from things that would keep you from becoming like our King—Jesus.

_____   _____
SIGNATURE   DATE

ANGELS UNSEEN

I PROMISE I Will Always Pray For You

Another angel, who had a gold container for incense, came and stood at the altar. This one was given a lot of incense to offer with the prayers of God's people on the gold altar in front of the throne. Then the smoke of the incense, together with the prayers of God's people, went up to God from the hand of the angel.

REVELATION 8:3-4

Carrie's knees were as tired as her head. Kneeling at her bedside for prayer time was the last thing she felt like doing. What she really wanted to do was put a wad of chewing gum in Brittany's hair. Earlier in the day in the school cafeteria, Brittany had called her names and threatened to gang up on her at recess. Carrie felt angry. More than that, she felt scared.

But it was bedtime now, and Carrie's frightened feelings would just have to be shoved aside. Besides, it was also time to pray. Her mother, seated on the edge of the bed, was watching. So with a slight huff, Carrie folded her hands and bowed her head. "Dear Lord, bless Mom and Daddy and Grandma and . . . and everybody else. Amen!" With a spurt of energy, she hopped to her feet and bounced into bed.

Her mother gave her one of those funny looks, almost a hurt look that said, *Is that it? That's all you want to pray?*

Carrie squirmed. She didn't want to think about Brittany again. And she certainly didn't want to pray about her.

"Carrie," her mom said, "are you sure there's nothing else you want to mention in your prayers?"

Carrie cupped her hand in her chin and silently shook her head no. She hated it whenever she said something—or didn't say something—that disappointed her mom. Even worse, this wasn't about not feeding the cat or putting away her clothes; this was about her inside feelings. More importantly, this was about prayer.

"Mom," she whined, "God knows what I'm going to pray anyway. Besides, I'm just a kid. My prayers are so . . . little."

Carrie's mother did what she always did when her daughter had questions about something important. She moved closer, fingered Carrie's long hair, and began to gently weave a braid. "Honey, no prayer is ever, ever too little."

Carrie thought hard about that as she relaxed under her mother's touch. *I want to believe it . . . really . . . but how do I know? Does God really care that I'm scared to walk into the cafeteria tomorrow? Or go outside for recess?*

Suddenly she straightened and asked her mother point-blank, "Mom, what does happen when I pray?"

At that exact instant, in a place far away yet closer than either mother or child could imagine, someone else was asking the very same question. A very unusual someone. An angel. An angel who, for the first time that very night, was taking on an important assignment. Zephyr was his name, and his new task was to tend to the prayers of God's children. A task that, he was soon to discover, was one of the most honored, privileged, and glorious assignments to which an angel could possibly be appointed.

But you couldn't convince Zephyr of that. Not that he wanted a better position in a more important legion of angels—coveting was completely unknown to him, as it was to all God's ministering spirits. It's just that he had . . . questions. And since part of his new assignment included overseeing the prayers of children Carrie's age, it was no wonder that her question just seconds earlier had caught his ear.

He leaned forward over time and space to edge just a tad closer to the bedroom to hear more. Carrie was murmuring something to her mother, something about being frightened in a cafeteria, or some such thing. It was hard for Zephyr to hear everything she was saying. *Oh, bother,* he thought, *I just wish she'd quit talking about it and start praying!* It always seemed to Zephyr that when boys and girls prayed, their words were far easier to hear, more sharp, crisp, and clear than ordinary talk about feeding cats, folding clothes, and fights in cafeterias.

The angel cupped his ear and listened closely. He recognized the next voice as that of Carrie's mother. "When you say a prayer, Carrie, it doesn't disappear into thin air. It has a special place in heaven where it goes. God listens . . . and all the angels are standing on tiptoe listening. So why don't we stop right now and pray about the things you've been telling me?"

Carrie was enjoying the soft voice of her mother, as well as their discussion, so she leaned over and sank her head into her mother's lap. Mom continued, "Let's believe together right now that your prayer is not too small, that God does care, and that things will change."

Up on the other side of time and space, Zephyr scratched his head in wonder. Oh, he knew that things changed when great preachers and missionaries prayed. He knew their prayers weren't small. He should. His last assignment was to look out for the prayers of seasoned saints who got on their knees in jungles and convents and cathedrals and great pulpits. He knew what happened when these great men and women prayed—important things happened. But boys and girls? Kids like Carrie who could only pray, "God bless Mommy"? Zephyr shook his head.

He sighed and turned to his larger, more experienced companion, Astar, a bright and beautiful angel who, Zephyr thought whenever he looked at him, had a winsome smile that was wise and yet very young. Zephyr cleared his throat and asked his friend, "So what *does* happen when a child prays?" He wasn't asking rudely, for that wasn't permitted either in the ranks of angels around the golden altar before the throne of God. But Zephyr knew that Astar would understand.

Astar smiled in his wise way, and then he, too, leaned forward to peer across time and space right through the ceiling into Carrie's bedroom. "My friend, if only you and that little girl there knew, really knew how important, how necessary . . ." The older angel's voice trailed off almost wistfully as he looked lovingly at Carrie who at this point was completely relaxed on her mother's lap, thoroughly enjoying the braiding and their talk.

Suddenly, time and space shifted slightly, and Astar and Zephyr saw a familiar glow coming toward them. Quickly, they got ready and stood waiting for it. A prayer was rising to the golden altar. As the two kept their eyes on Carrie's bedroom, they knew right away where the prayer came from. As the glowing ember rose, Zephyr could hear the sound of Carrie's voice all pure and perfect, with a dash more wisdom than usual. "Dear Lord, help me not to be afraid . . ." And then came another prayer which, Zephyr and Astar noticed, was mixed with a mother's voice as well: "Thy kingdom come; Thy will be done on earth as it is in heaven."

"Ah, this is very special." Astar smiled broadly as Zephyr cradled the prayer and turned toward the golden altar before the throne. "A parent and child praying together! Our Master who is the heavenly Father of this mother and child will be very glad to add their prayer with the perfume of the incense." The two angels glanced over their shoulders toward Carrie's bedroom. Both mother and child were close to each other and still praying. The two angels paused with prayer-in-hand to watch in amazement the glorious power that surrounded Carrie and her mom as they clasped their hands together. And as they prayed, Astar and Zephyr noticed that the prayer that they were carefully cradling glowed brighter. The two angels continued their path toward the golden altar.

"All ranks stand at attention!" came an angelic shout from the center of the legion. For as far as you could see, angels upon angels upon angels stretched out in row after row around the golden altar before the throne. And as far as you could tell, every single angel was standing tall, respectful of Astar and Zephyr as they approached the altar.

An angel close to the throne of the Father announced with great joy, "One of the Master's children and her mother are offering a prayer before the throne! Listen one and all: The prayer before their Father and their great Savior, the Lord Jesus Christ, is that the kingdom of the Almighty here in heaven, this great kingdom of peace and joy, will find its way into their hearts, as well as into the hearts of those for whom they pray. May it be done on earth as it is in heaven!"

Then the gentle, yet powerful voice of the Father spoke; actually it beamed, sounding less like words and more like brilliant light. "What a wise prayer," the Father said happily, "and it shall be done because it honors My will."

Zephyr was amazed. It was as if the entire universe had braked to a halt. The throne room was so caught up in dignified silence that you could have heard a string break—boing!—on a harp. That little tiny prayer of Carrie's was commanding all this attention?

The Father continued speaking. "What's more, this child will help me reach another little one—little Brittany."

Zephyr was overwhelmed with a deep sense of joyous responsibility. As he and Astar came up to the altar, Zephyr nodded to the angels on one side, then the other. Just as Astar and Zephyr were about to mix the prayer of Carrie and her mother with incense, the older angel leaned over and whispered to his friend, "Now do you see?"

With a different kind of heavenly tears in his eyes, Zephyr said softly, "Yes, I see. Let the little children draw close to the Father, for of such is the kingdom of heaven. The Master loves children. He loves it when they pray."

As the two angels poured the prayer upon the altar, a great rumbling began in the heavenlies. The floor of the throne room shook, and every angel in every rank and legion bowed low. The kingdom of heaven was, at that moment, shifting and being yanked, even if ever so slightly, toward earth. Carrie's prayer was at that instant being answered.

Right then Carrie's mother cocked her head, sensing that something in the room had changed. She smiled knowingly as she slid her near-sleeping child from her lap to the bed and whispered, "I believe something's different, don't you, Carrie?"

The little girl, happy and half-asleep, and still feeling warm from her mother's touch, voice, and their prayer together, reached up and hugged her mom. "I'm not afraid, Mom . . . I love you."

Carrie's mother flicked off the bedside lamp and leaned down to kiss her daughter. It was one of those moments she didn't want to end; and as Carrie reached from under the covers and squeezed her hand, it was clear that something special had happened between them. An overwhelming sense of peace and a deep, unexplainable kind of joy filled the room as it filled their hearts. Especially Carrie's heart. For both of them, the moment felt as though it had been sent straight from heaven.

Zephyr and Astar smiled at one another. It had.

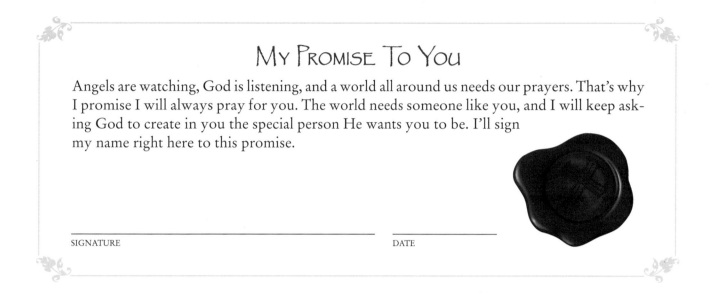

My Promise To You

Angels are watching, God is listening, and a world all around us needs our prayers. That's why I promise I will always pray for you. The world needs someone like you, and I will keep asking God to create in you the special person He wants you to be. I'll sign my name right here to this promise.

_____   _____

SIGNATURE   DATE

ALWAYS

I PROMISE I WILL ALWAYS LOVE YOU

Love is always supportive, loyal, hopeful, and trusting.

1 CORINTHIANS 13:7

I hate this," Carl said aloud as he got into his car. His was the only one left in the parking lot of the TV studio where he worked. It had been a bad day, one in a parade of bad days. In less than a year, he had gone from being the best in the business to the joke of the town. No one bought his ideas anymore. Today was the beginning of his last chance.

"You've got a month, Sheridan," his boss had told him. "One month to deliver a story we can sell to the networks. Make it a love story. You know, something for Valentine's Day next year. All I want from you is an outline. Think you can do that, Sheridan?"

"Yes, sir," Carl had answered the boss's sneer. "Count on it. I'll find you the greatest love story ever written!"

"Cut the speeches, Sheridan. Just do it or else . . ."

As Carl drove home that night, he thought about what it would be like to lose his job. He thought about the money. About the embarrassment. About his family.

Some family, he thought as he pulled into the driveway. *A fourteen-year-old vegetable propped up in a chair and a wife who's more a nurse than a wife.*

His son, Michael, had suffered brain damage in a bicycle accident three years earlier. The family had set off on an innocent ride to the school parking lot one day, but a delivery van lost control and shattered the innocence. Life stopped for Carl then. Each day seemed to bring some new problem. *What will it be today?* a voice seemed to whisper. *A seizure? Pneumonia? Bed sores?*

Carl pulled his car into the garage and sat for a moment in silence.

"I hate this," he said.

"How was work today?" Nancy asked as she and Carl began supper that night.

"Fine."

"Just fine?"

"I guess."

"Tell me."

"Tell you what?"

"Why it was just fine and not great."

Carl groaned to himself at the thought of telling her what had happened. He was ashamed and afraid.

"Just a dumb assignment, that's all. I need to find a love story."

"That doesn't sound too bad. There's plenty to choose from—don't you think?"

"That's just the problem. There are too many to choose from. Every story's been done before. Nothing new." Carl stopped there, not wanting to tell her what was at stake if he could not find a good story—a great story. He took a second helping of rice, signaling the end of the conversation. The two sat in silence again until a voice came from the opposite end of the house.

"What was that?" Carl asked.

"What?"

"That voice?"

"Oh, that's Michael. He's playing with his new toy. Didn't you see it when you stopped by his room?"

"Ah, no. I mean . . ." Carl had not stopped by the room to see Michael.

"It's not really a toy," Nancy explained. "You type words on the keyboard, and then the computer voice speaks them out."

"Michael's typing?" Carl asked in unbelief.

"No, of course not. His therapist at the Center typed in some words, but Michael learned to push the play button. She programmed it to say, 'I love you.' Isn't that sweet?"

"Yeah, sweet." Carl decided to hold his tongue and not give his wife the same speech he'd given her a hundred times before. He didn't like anyone doing "sweet" things with Michael, as if the boy were a pet.

Nancy went to get Michael while Carl continued eating. She pushed his bulky wheelchair into the dining room and parked it at the right of her chair.

Michael looked like a starving child from some famine-stricken country. His skin clung tightly to bones that bent at odd angles, stiff and twisted. His arms and hands dangled in the air and made him look like a praying mantis. His face was locked in a look of shock, as if he were still seeing the van that hit him, bearing down on him from above.

"Daddy's home," Nancy said to him as she wiped his mouth.

Michael seemed to ignore her as his attention wandered to the keyboard again, and he moved his hand like a giant crane over the pad. His finger came down on the play button. "I love you," the machine said.

"I love you, too," Nancy said as she put her face close to his and held his hand. She looked back for Carl's response. "He loves us," she said hopefully.

"Seems like the therapist taught him a neat trick," was the best Carl could muster.

"I love you," the machine said again.

"It's not a trick, Carl." Nancy turned back to him. "They just want him to be a part of the Valentine's Day program, and they thought he'd enjoy it. They love him, honey, that's all."

"I love you."

"Tell him to stop, will you?" Carl pleaded. "In fact, tell those people to leave my kid alone. Tell them . . . tell them he's not their toy. And take that dumb machine back to . . ."

"I love you." Michael continued pushing the button.

". . . the store. It's a waste of money. He doesn't know what it's for!"

"I love you."

"Turn it off, I said!" Carl yelled as he slammed his fist on the table. Michael jerked his hand back in fear. Nancy looked away from Carl and held Michael's arms.

"It's okay, honey. Daddy's had a bad day. No more talking, okay?" She took the board off the top of his tray and placed it beside his leg.

Michael relaxed just long enough to start a low, eerie groan. It was a cry of defiance. Or sadness. They could never tell which. Whatever it meant, Carl knew it would last a long time.

"I've had enough," he said quietly and left the table.

❧

Carl spent three long weeks on his search for the perfect love story. But in the end he could only put together a story that seemed no different from any other love story he'd seen. He could only hope his boss would be fooled.

The boss was not fooled.

"Three and a half weeks, and this is all I get?" Carl's boss tossed the outline back across the desk. "It's too bad, Carl. You were the best."

"But, sir—"

"No, Sheridan. Time's up. This is a tough business, and we need someone with drive and talent. Nothing personal—understand?"

"Yeah," Carl said. He turned and walked away without argument. He roamed the city for hours.

❦

"You're late," Nancy said as Carl walked in from the garage that night just before nine. "And you promised."

"Promised what?"

"You promised to be at Michael's Valentine's Day program this afternoon, remember?"

Carl winced. "Why didn't you call to remind me?"

"I did, but they said you'd gone already. Where were you?"

"Just out," Carl answered as he put his coat away. It was obvious no one at the office had told her what had happened. He was relieved and decided to keep it that way.

"Well, I'd love to stay and make you feel guiltier, but I've got to leave for the grocery store before it closes. Don't forget to look in on Michael, will you? I think he knows you weren't at the program." Nancy turned and left.

Carl stood alone in the hallway. The sounds of her leaving—the door slamming, the whining engine of the car in reverse—triggered a choice for Carl. He would do the same. But he would leave for good.

It's over, he thought.

He was surprised at how quickly he made the choice, but he knew it was what he had to do. He hurried to his room where he changed into his jeans, a sweatshirt, and then shoved some clothes into a suitcase. He would stay in a hotel nearby. Just one night. Then . . . the rest was a blank, but he would figure that out later. He finished packing and wrote a quick note:

Nancy,
I lost my job today. Not much left for me here either. I just can't accept what happened to Michael . . . to us. I feel like I've lost you both. I'll call you.
Carl

He laid the note on the bed and walked down the hall to Michael's room. Michael was in the corner staring at the ceiling. Carl stopped in the doorway and, for what seemed like the first time in three years, spoke directly to his son.

"I'm done, kid. I've got no job. And your mom's not happy. And I'm not much of a dad to you. Others find a way to be happy with the way you are, but I can't. It's nothing personal, understand? It's just that . . ."

Michael's eyes flickered for a moment, and his head began a slow cocking to one side, as if to search for the voice that was speaking to him.

"I'm gonna go. Mom will take good care of you. And so will the people at the Center. They love you."

Carl turned and walked away. As he did so, he heard the faint sound of clicking coming from Michael's room—a slow click followed by a long pause, then another slow click.

"Dumb toy," he mumbled as he continued toward the garage.

He was in the kitchen when the end came. It came with a word, a word he'd not heard for the longest time. He strained his ears in disbelief. Was it true? Could it be possible? Was Michael really talking to him?

He heard the word again. It gripped his heart as if to stop it. His head spun. Tears burst from his eyes. He dropped his bag and sank to the floor, sobbing softly as he sat in the dark.

The clicking began again.

I can't leave, Carl thought. *I should have never thought of leaving. Even if I'm dreaming all this, I have to stay.* He stopped his thinking, afraid that he would not hear the word again.

In his room, Michael aimed his bony finger once more at the keyboard, straining to form the words he had held in his heart for so long. The nasal, flat voice of the computer echoed down the hall to bring—to keep—the prodigal home forever.

"Daddy, I love you."

MY PROMISE TO YOU

Love finds a way to love forever, no matter how much hurt you feel. It keeps its promises. It doesn't let go, and I won't let go either. I'm signing my name here so you can remind me in case I forget. And in case you forget, too, on those days when you hurt inside.

_____   _____
SIGNATURE   DATE

THE PRODIGAL

I PROMISE I WILL ALWAYS FORGIVE YOU

Be kind and compassionate to one another, forgiving each other,
just as in Christ God forgave you.

EPHESIANS 4:32

L isa sat on the floor of her old room, staring at the box that lay in front of her. It was an old shoe box that she had decorated to become a memory box many years before. Stickers and penciled flowers covered the top and sides. Its edges were worn, the corners of the lid taped so as to keep their shape.

It had been three years since Lisa last opened the box. A sudden move to Boston had kept her from packing it. But now that she was back home, she took the time to look again at the memories. Fingering the corners of the box and stroking its cover, Lisa pictured in her mind what was inside.

There was a photo of the family trip to the Grand Canyon, a note from her friend telling her that Nick Bicotti liked her, and the Indian arrowhead she had found while on her senior class trip.

One by one, she remembered the items in the box, lingering over the sweetest, until she came to the last and only painful memory. She knew what it looked like—a single sheet of paper upon which lines had been drawn to form boxes, 490 of them to be exact. And each box contained a check mark, one for each time.

❧

"How many times must I forgive my brother?" the disciple Peter had asked Jesus. "Seven times?"

Lisa's Sunday school teacher had read Jesus' surprise answer to the class. "Seventy times seven."

Lisa had leaned over to her brother Brent as the teacher continued reading.

"How many times is that?" she whispered.

Brent, though two years younger, was smarter than she was.

"Four hundred and ninety," Brent wrote on the corner of his Sunday school paper.

Lisa saw the message, nodded, and sat back in her chair. She watched her brother as the lesson continued. He was small for his age, with narrow shoulders and short arms. His glasses were too large for his face, and his hair always matted in swirls. He bordered on being a nerd, but his incredible skills at everything, especially music, made him popular with his classmates. Brent had learned to play the piano at age four, the clarinet at age seven, and had just begun playing the oboe. His music teachers said he'd be a famous musician someday.

There was only one thing at which Lisa was better than Brent—basketball. They played it almost every afternoon after school. Brent could have refused to play, but he knew that it was Lisa's only joy in the midst of her struggles to get C's and D's at school.

Lisa's attention came back to her Sunday school teacher as the woman finished the lesson and closed with prayer.

That same Sunday afternoon found brother and sister playing basketball in the driveway. It was then that the counting had begun. Brent was guarding Lisa as she dribbled toward the basket. He had tried to bat the ball away, got his face near her elbow, and took a shot on the chin.

"Ow!" he cried out and turned away.

Lisa saw her opening and drove to the basket, making an easy lay-up. She gloated over her success but stopped when she saw Brent.

"You okay?" she asked.

Brent shrugged his shoulders.

"Sorry," Lisa said. "Really. It was a cheap shot."

"It's all right. I forgive you," he said. A thin smile then formed on his face. "Just 489 more times though."

"Whaddaya mean?" Lisa asked.

"You know . . . what we learned in Sunday school today. You're supposed to forgive someone 490 times. I just forgave you, so now you have 489 left," he kidded.

The two of them laughed at the thought of keeping track of every time Lisa had done something to Brent. They were sure she had gone past 490 long ago.

The rain interrupted their game, and the two moved indoors.

"Wanna play Battleship?" Lisa asked.

Brent agreed, and they were soon on the floor of the living room with their game boards in front of them. Each took turns calling out a letter and number combination, hoping to hit each other's ships.

Lisa knew she was in trouble as the game went on. Brent had only lost one ship out of five. Lisa had lost three. Desperate to win, she found herself leaning over the edge of Brent's barrier ever so slightly. She was thus able to see where Brent had placed two of his ships. She quickly evened the score.

Pleased, Lisa searched once more for the location of the last two ships. She peered over the barrier again, but this time Brent caught her in the act.

"Hey, you're cheating!" He stared at her in disbelief.

Lisa's face turned red. Her lips quivered. "I'm sorry," she said, staring at the carpet.

There was not much Brent could say. He knew Lisa sometimes did things like this. He felt sorry that Lisa found so few things she could do well. It was wrong for her to cheat, but he knew the temptation was hard for her.

"Okay, I forgive you," Brent said. Then he added with a small laugh, "I guess it's down to 488 now, huh?"

"Yeah, I guess so." She returned his kindness with a weak smile and added, "Thanks for being my brother, Brent."

Brent's forgiving spirit gripped Lisa, and she wanted him to know how sorry she was. It was that evening that she had made the chart with the 490 boxes. She showed it to him before he went to bed. "We can keep track of every time I mess up and you forgive me," she said. "See? I'll put a check in each box—like this." She placed two marks in the upper left-hand boxes. "These are for today."

Brent raised his hands to protest. "You don't need to keep—"

"Yes, I do!" Lisa interrupted. "You're always forgiving me, and I want to keep track. Just let me do this!" She went back to her room and tacked the chart to her bulletin board.

There were many opportunities to fill in the chart in the years that followed. She once told the kids at school that Brent talked in his sleep and called out Rhonda Hill's name, even though it wasn't true. The teasing caused Brent days and days of misery. When she realized how cruel she had been, Lisa apologized sincerely. That night she marked box number 96.

Forgiveness number 211 came in the tenth grade when Lisa failed to bring home his English book. Brent had stayed home sick that day and had asked her to bring it so he could study for a quiz. She forgot and he got a C.

Number 393 was for the lost keys . . . 418 for the extra bleach she put in the washer, which ruined his favorite polo shirt . . . 449, the dent she had put in his car when she had borrowed it.

There was a small ceremony when Lisa checked number 490. She used a gold pen for the check mark, had Brent sign the chart, and then placed it in her memory box.

"I guess that's the end," Lisa said. "No more screw-ups from me anymore!"

Brent just laughed. "Yeah, right."

Number 491 was just another one of Lisa's careless mistakes, but its hurt lasted a lifetime. Brent had become all that his music teachers said he would. Few could play the oboe better than he. In his fourth year at the best music school in the United States, he received the opportunity of a lifetime—a chance to try out for New York City's great orchestra. The tryout would be held sometime during the following two weeks. It would be the fulfillment of his young dreams. But he never got the chance.

Brent had been out when the call about the tryout came to the house. Lisa was the only one home and on her way out the door, eager to get to work on time.

"Two-thirty on the tenth," the secretary said on the phone.

Lisa did not have a pen, but she told herself that she could remember it. "Got it. Thanks," she answered. *I can remember that,* she thought. But she did not.

It was a week later around the dinner table that Lisa realized her mistake.

"So, Brent," his mom asked him, "when do you try out?"

"Don't know yet. They're supposed to call."

Lisa froze in her seat.

"Oh, no!" she blurted out loud. "What's today's date? Quick!"

"It's the twelfth," her dad answered. "Why?"

A terrible pain ripped through Lisa's heart. She buried her face in her hands, crying.

"Lisa, what's the matter?" her mother asked.

Through sobs Lisa explained what had happened. "It was two days ago . . . the tryout . . . two-thirty . . . the call came . . . last week."

Brent sat back in his chair, not believing Lisa.

"Is this one of your jokes, sis?" he asked, though he could tell her misery was real.

She shook her head, still unable to look at him.

"Then I really missed it?"

She nodded.

Brent ran out of the kitchen without a word. He did not come out of his room the rest of the evening. Lisa tried once to knock on the door, but she could not face him. She went to her room where she cried bitterly.

Suddenly she knew what she had to do. She had ruined Brent's life. He could never forgive her for that. She had failed her family, and there was nothing to do but to leave home.

Lisa packed her pickup truck in the middle of the night and left a note behind, telling her folks she'd be all right. She began writing a note to Brent, but her words sounded empty to her. *Nothing I say could make a difference anyway,* she thought.

Two days later she got a job as a waitress in Boston. She found an apartment not too far from the restaurant.

Her parents tried many times to reach her, but Lisa ignored their letters. "It's too late," she wrote them once. "I've ruined Brent's life, and I'm not coming back."

Lisa did not think she would ever see home again. But one day in the restaurant where she worked, she saw a face she knew.

"Lisa!" said Mrs. Nelson, looking up from her plate. "What a surprise." The woman was a friend of Lisa's family from back home.

"I was so sorry to hear about your brother," Mrs. Nelson said softly. "Such a terrible accident. But we can be thankful that he died quickly. He didn't suffer."

Lisa stared at the woman in shock. "Wh-hat," she finally stammered. It couldn't be! Her brother? Dead?

The woman quickly saw that Lisa did not know about the accident. She told the girl the sad story of the speeding car, the rush to the hospital, the doctors working over Brent. But all they could do was not enough to save him.

Lisa returned home that afternoon.

Now she found herself in her room thinking about her brother as she held the small box that held some of her memories of him. Sadly, she opened the box and peered inside. It was as she remembered, except for one item—Brent's chart. It was not there. In its place, at the bottom of the box, was an envelope. Her hands shook as she tore it open and removed a letter. The first page read:

> *Dear Lisa,*
> *It was you who kept count, not me. But if you're stubborn enough to keep count, use the new chart I've made for you.*
> *Love, Brent*

Lisa turned to the second page where she found a chart just like the one she had made as a child, but on this one the lines were drawn in perfect precision. And unlike the chart she had kept, there was but one check mark in the upper left-hand corner. Written in red felt tip pen over the entire page were the words:

"Number 491. Forgiven, forever."

My Promise To You

I promise I will always forgive you. And I won't keep count. God's not good at math when it comes to our sins, and neither am I. I love you too much.

_____   _____
SIGNATURE   DATE

HEAVENLY HELP

I PROMISE I WILL ALWAYS BE THERE FOR YOU

The Lord your God will always be at your side, and he will never abandon you.

DEUTERONOMY 31:6

Justin William Chase, Jr., leaned around the half-opened door of his father's study. Actually, it wasn't so much a study as an art studio. And whenever the hallway smelled like turpentine and oil paint, Justin could tell that his father was about to begin work on a new painting.

Sure enough, Justin William Chase, Sr., in his long paint-splattered smock, was turning a large easel in the direction of the sunlight that streamed through the tall window. Next to the easel was a small table covered with bottles and brushes, tubes, paint rags, and several palettes. Justin, who wanted nothing more than to be a famous painter like his father, saw his chance to have fun.

"Father," he said as he ran into the room, "may I help you get ready?" Justin reached for a couple of the tubes of paint and began to put them in neat little rows.

"Better than that," Mr. Chase said with a smile, "why don't you bring my stool over and sit up here on my knee?"

That was exactly what the little boy was hoping his father would say. Within minutes, Justin was doing his favorite thing in his favorite place. He was sitting on his father's lap before a huge canvas in the studio of Boston's most famous artist of the 1800s: his dad. What's more, his dad was letting him paint.

Nothing thrilled Justin more than to hold one of his father's brushes. Mr. Chase would then wrap his large hand around Justin's and dab the brush into the paint on the palette. Holding on to his son's hand and the brush, the artist would swirl the most beautiful colors across the canvas. Justin, all wide-eyed and grinning, delighted in feeling his father's hand around his. More so, he thrilled to see the canvas begin to fill with red and blue and yellow.

He was painting! Actually, his father was doing the painting, but from Justin's point of view, it was hard to tell the difference. He didn't know which was more fun: creating something beautiful right before his eyes or sitting on his dad's knee and feeling the warmth and gentle pressure of his father's hand. The little boy really didn't care. All he cared about was being with his dad and feeling important, safe, and secure.

With such care and good training, it was no surprise that within a matter of years Justin William Chase, Jr., was enrolled in one of the finest art schools in New England. His teachers were amazed at their young student's talent. Once, while watching Justin angle his brush a certain way on the canvas, one of his teachers remarked, "How did you become so skilled with the brush?"

The young man turned and, with smudges of paint on his chin, thought for a moment, looking off in a dreamy way. He said softly, "I can almost feel my dad's hand around mine when I paint." Justin then shook his head, as if coming out of a dream. "My father is getting older, but he's still the best painter in the world. And one day," he added with resolve, "I will be famous just like him!"

And it was true. His father was very famous (although he cared little about fame and fortune; he simply delighted in being a good painter). The old artist would say to his son, "Justin, don't make fame your goal. Just enjoy the gift God has given you. Paint for Him and give of yourself wherever He places you."

"Yes, Father." Justin would nod obediently, but when he was back at school, flipping through art books, and happened to see a page with one of his father's paintings on it, he'd swell with pride. Yes, Justin Chase, Jr., would one day go to Paris to study and become a great painter—a famous painter—like his father.

Finally, the day arrived when Mr. Chase stood with his grown son on the Boston docks next to a big steamship about to sail for Europe. Justin put down his suitcases and hugged his aging father. He was surprised at how frail and thin the older man seemed. Justin hated leaving him.

The trip across the Atlantic Ocean took many days. Sometimes on windy afternoons, Justin would walk to the stern of the boat, lean on the ship's rail, and look back toward America. Oh, how he missed his father and how he hoped he was feeling better. Then Justin would walk forward to the bow and feel the wind in his face. He would think about Europe and Paris and attending the best art school in the world.

Paris was even better than he had imagined. Every day he and his fellow students visited museums and galleries or took long field trips out into the French countryside. They would take out their sketch pads at every chance, perhaps stopping by a stream to discuss how to paint the water that gurgled and splashed over rocks. Justin always seemed to have an idea. "I think that since water moves fast," he would say, "you should paint it fast and not be too careful. Like this . . ." And then he would quickly and artfully sketch the stream. It was perfect. His skill did not go unnoticed. Justin was quickly becoming known not only among the students, but among the art experts.

Many letters passed back and forth between Paris and Boston. As time went by, Justin noticed that his father's handwriting was becoming more scribbly and hard to read. But always, somewhere in the letters, the old painter would write, "Son, I believe in you. I am here if you ever need me." Those words always brought a tear to Justin's eyes. He would carefully fold his father's letters and then turn to his art and work even harder.

It was this commitment that won Justin such fame among the gallery owners in Paris. And not just Paris, but throughout all of Europe. Well-known art collectors began to seek out the paintings of Justin William Chase, Jr. Justin wrote long letters to his father, explaining that now his works were hanging in the finest palaces throughout all of France and beyond while requests for his paintings were constantly pouring in.

But fame and fortune took its toll. "Where is my painting?" demanded a wealthy collector who stormed into Justin's studio one day.

But he had to stand in line. Others were ahead of him asking, "When will you finish my order?" and "I thought you would have my painting framed by now!"

Justin could only turn to his work and paint as fast and furiously as he could. He never realized there would be so much pressure and disappointment connected with being famous. Sometimes, in the middle of a painting, he would wonder, *My father was famous, but he was happy. Why am I so sad?*

Back in America, the old painter sensed something wrong. For one thing, there were fewer letters than in earlier days. For another, the art critics were beginning to question the works of the young artist who, as they wrote, "will never be as good as his father."

The old artist sighed and sent a message. "My son, come home," and then added with emphasis, "come home before it's too late."

When the message arrived, Justin was shocked. "Come home before it's too late," he read. What did this mean? Was his father's health worse? Bewildered, he put the letter down and looked around his studio. There were no longer lines of people clamoring for his works. Surrounding him were piles of unfinished paintings and blank canvases. He was afraid he would never be able to paint a beautiful painting again. He glanced again at his dad's message, and tears filled his eyes. *I've lost my talent—and now I might lose my father.* The following day Justin booked passage on the next steamship back to America.

Arriving in Boston, Justin hurried home, caught his breath, and then quietly walked into the familiar study. His father, frail and leaning on a cane, sat on his stool near one of the old easels. Sunlight streamed in and bathed the old man in a warm glow. Justin shut the door behind him. "I've been waiting for you," the painter said with a smile.

"Oh, Father," Justin cried as he walked over and knelt by the stool. "I'm not too late. You're all right."

"Yes, everything's all right. And, my son, it's not too late for you either. I have heard about your work. About your—"

"Father, I'm so ashamed. After all these years, I have finally realized that I don't have your gift. I'll never be the artist you are." Justin buried his head against his father's knee.

The old painter placed his hand on his son's head. "Dear Justin, I don't care if you are ever famous. I only care that you become all that God intends you to be; and for this, my child, it is not too late. Here. Come with me to my easel."

Justin walked arm-in-arm with his father over to one of the large blank canvases. They stood there for a moment, and then the old man said, "Reach for one of my brushes, son."

Justin held the brush up in his hand, and the next thing he knew, his father was standing behind him and had wrapped his thin hand around his. Suddenly he was a child again, feeling his arm lift and stretch as together, under his father's strength, they splashed and dabbed paint on the canvas. It was just two hands on a single brush, swirling and stroking and filling the entire canvas with beautiful color.

"Oh, this is wonderful!" Justin laughed out loud. "I haven't had this much fun in years!" In less than an hour, father and son stood before the most beautiful painting Justin had ever seen.

"Father, look at what you did. It's amazing! After all this time, you've only gotten better. Do you see this?" He turned to the old man. He paused for a moment and was struck by the way the sun touched his father's face. The golden rays washed away the age and wrinkles, and Justin felt as though he were seeing a side of his father he had never known before. He roused from his thoughts and said one more time, "Father, look . . . do you see what you've done while guiding my hand?"

There was a long silence. And then, very slowly, the old painter spoke. "No, Justin, I can't see. I am almost blind. I cannot see the canvas."

His son slowly shook his head in disbelief. "How?" he stammered. He turned to the painting. "How did you do this if you can't see?"

"Justin, *you* did it. The gift never left you. All you needed to overcome your fear was to feel my touch and to know my presence and love for you—to know *God's* love and presence. Fame—even failure—can make a person forget things like that. This is why I wanted you to come home. It wasn't for my sake." The old man wrapped his arms around his boy. "It was for your sake."

Justin held his father as tightly as he could and cried. Not with sad tears or tears of regret, but tears of relief and joy.

"Give of yourself wherever God places you," the old artist said as he patted his son's shoulder. His blind eyes became wet, too, when he added, "And remember, for as long as He allows, my hand will always be near to guide you."

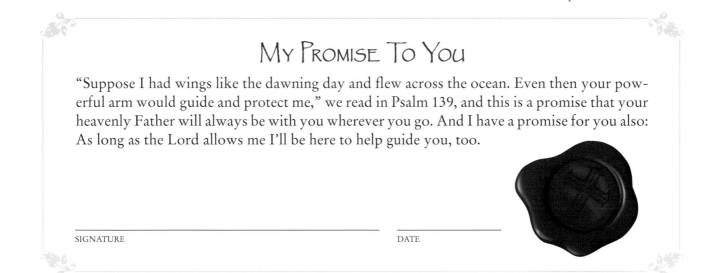

My Promise To You

"Suppose I had wings like the dawning day and flew across the ocean. Even then your powerful arm would guide and protect me," we read in Psalm 139, and this is a promise that your heavenly Father will always be with you wherever you go. And I have a promise for you also: As long as the Lord allows me I'll be here to help guide you, too.

_____   _____
SIGNATURE   DATE

TRUTH

I PROMISE I WILL ALWAYS TELL YOU THE TRUTH

You will know the truth, and the truth will set you free.

JOHN 8:32

amp, dark, scary and, oh, so cold. That's exactly what Christopher thought of the cavernous rooms and tunnels of the underground world in which he lived. And that's exactly why he faithfully kept the lamps lit along the passageways that linked the home of his family with the homes of all the other cave dwellers.

"I am *not* afraid of the dark. . . . I am not afraid of the dark," Christopher said out loud as he lifted his long wooden pole to reach the lantern on the side of the wall. His voice echoed down the corridor. He could hear other cave dwellers lighting lamps in distant districts throughout the underground city. Their oil lanterns threw off flashes of light against the far end of the tunnel. He shivered and continued his work of lighting the lamps.

"I'm tired of being afraid . . . and I hate this stupid darkness," he mumbled as he made his way back to the cluster of red clay rooms where he lived with his mother, sisters, and grandfather. When he arrived home, he dusted the dirt from the cave off his shoes and entered the central room where his family was gathering for a meal. Christopher threw down his pole in frustration. "Isn't there anything we can do to get rid of this darkness? This awful cold?"

Christopher and his mother had been over it time and again. He really didn't expect a different answer. And again the same old reply came: "This is the way it is, Christopher. This is the way our people have always lived. The cold and dark only remind us of how important it is to carry on the Work of the Lamps. We must not let the lanterns in the tunnels go out, or else the darkness will overtake us."

This answer never satisfied Christopher. How could anyone be satisfied living in constant fear and cold? As the boy warmed his hands against the glowing stove, he glanced at his grandfather. It seemed to Christopher that the old man was never satisfied with that answer either. Unlike Christopher, though, his grandfather never spoke up.

That is, until tonight. The old man leaned back in his chair. "Yes, there *is* something that can be done about the darkness. There is a better light. A greater light. This is not," he said as he pointed toward the flame-flickered embers, "the only light there is." Dishes stopped clattering, and knives and forks were stilled. Everyone was stunned into silence. Even Christopher.

His mother fluffed her apron as if to say something important. "Father, you are mistaken," she said as politely as possible. "There is no other light than the one we know here in the caves. Besides, it is impossible to know otherwise. We must work hard to keep the lamps of our city lit, for if we don't, darkness will indeed overwhelm us, and we shall surely die." The little girls, with hands folded, nodded obediently. But when the boy's eyes met his grandfather's, Christopher realized his sisters were the only ones who believed it.

Later, after the lamps were tended and everyone was asleep, Christopher crept into his grandfather's room. The old man was sitting in the glow of a candle with a magnifying glass, straining to read the words in a large book. The boy pulled up a stool and said softly, "Tell me, please, tell me the truth. Tell me about the great light."

For a long moment his grandfather did not reply but only squinted closer at the page. Then he spoke. "Learn the riddle of our ancestors, my son."

> "'*Seek the Light you cannot see,*
> *The Light of God that guideth thee.*
> *Do not fear the dark and damp.*
> *Fear instead the man-made lamp.*'"

With that, he closed the book, took the candle in one hand, and grabbed Christopher's hand with the other. "We must make our way to the Great Hall immediately," Grandfather instructed.

Together they hurried through the twisting tunnels and cobblestone passageways until they arrived at a huge wooden door lit by torches on either side. The old man wiped away a thick layer of soot on the stone above the door. Carved in the rock was the same riddle.

Christopher whispered, "Grandfather, what does it mean when it says, 'Seek the Light you cannot see'? And the part that says, 'Do not fear the dark and damp. Fear instead the man-made lamp'?" The old man did not reply, but rather led him into the grand chamber carved out of rock. A large table stood in the middle. Small oil lamps flickered on either wall. "Is this where the great light is?" Christopher asked.

The eyes of the old man twinkled. "You will see." With that, he reached for the first lamp on the wall, cupped his hand, and—

"Grandfather! What are you doing?" Christopher grabbed for his arm, but it was too late. His grandfather had done the unthinkable. He had blown out a lamp! And then he blew out another. And another. Darkness, thick and black like nothing Christopher had ever seen, filled the room. Had his grandfather played a trick on him? Scared stiff, the boy jumped to his feet.

"You don't need to be afraid of the dark anymore," came his grandfather's calm voice out of the blackness. "Here," the old man said as he reached for the boy and pulled him close to his side. Christopher buried his face in the old man's shoulder. "Open your eyes," his grandfather said, ". . . and look for the Light you cannot see."

Christopher blinked and squinted into the middle of the Great Hall. He rubbed his eyes and looked closer, focusing on something he had never seen before. "Ye-e-es," he said, feeling the fear drain out of his body. "I see it!"

"And you are no longer afraid, are you?" his grandfather asked.

"It's strange, but no, I'm not," the boy said as he peered at the shadows in the room. "But, Grandfather, why have you kept it a secret for so long?"

The old man sighed. "For many years I have looked for someone like you who hates the dark and the cold enough to risk everything . . . yes, everything, to change it. You are the one who is wise and brave enough to help others see the truth."

"Me? Wise and brave?" Christopher rose to his feet.

"Yes, and you must act now," Grandfather said as he placed his arm around his grandson's shoulder. They walked back into the passageway. The torches crackled, throwing eerie, flitting shadows on the walls. "The people will be awake soon. The men will be starting the Work of the Lamps in the tunnels. Go quickly and tell them the truth. Tell them what you've seen."

Christopher wasted no time. He raced down the corridor past the dying, flickering lanterns on the wall. He ran so fast that some of the flames blew out, but Christopher didn't slow down. He was no longer afraid of the dark. Finally, he came to the workers. The men were pouring oil into their lanterns to begin the Work of the Lamps. "Stop! Please! We don't have to do this anymore," the boy panted.

One of the leaders spoke up. "Aren't you the young lamplighter from the northwest tunnels? The one who complains about the cold and the dark?" Someone chuckled near the back of the line.

"Yes," Christopher huffed, "and I've discovered the truth. Something new, something wonderful!"

"That you can get warm by running to work?" another laughed.

"Here," a lamplighter jeered as he threw a pole at Christopher. "Light your lantern. We've wasted enough time. The oil in the lamps along the corridors is getting dangerously low. We have urgent work to do!"

Tears welled up in Christopher's eyes. He stammered and pleaded with the people. But they marched by and pushed him out of their way. They were about to disappear around the corner when suddenly he remembered his grandfather's words: "You are the one who hates the dark and cold enough to risk everything to change it."

That was all he needed. He tore off his shirt and knotted the sleeves around the end of a pole. Raising high his "flag," he swirled it over his head and whipped up a wind that blew out every freshly trimmed wall lamp within a hundred yards.

"Stop him!" the leaders of the lamplighters yelled.

But Christopher was way ahead, racing down the tunnel, blowing and beating out every lamp along the way. He shouted, "Don't be afraid of the dark! There's no need to be afraid!"

"Halt!" they yelled, running after him. "We will be smothered in the darkness! We will die of the cold!" Some picked up rocks. Others threw their poles like spears. The crowd grew and became a panicking wave surging up the tunnel. But the faster they rushed to catch the young boy, the more lamps were blown out by their draft. The tunnels went pitch-black.

Christopher, heaving and gasping, finally arrived at the Great Hall. When he reached his grandfather's side, he turned to face the angry crowd holding what few torches were left.

"This boy has ruined the Work of the Lamps! We are doomed in this darkness!" they yelled.

"Quick! Catch!" Grandfather said as he tossed a pole to his grandson. "Jump up on the table!" Christopher did as he was told and reached with the pole as high as he could. Stretching up in the near dark, he found a rusty ring on the underside of a trap door. He hooked the end of the pole on the ring, and with all his might he pulled and pulled until finally . . .

"Aaaah!" Christopher cried as a great stream of dazzling light flooded the entire room. Brilliance beamed everywhere, changing the entire cave dwelling into a glorious chamber of pure white light. Standing there, slightly dazed, they all rubbed their eyes and lifted their faces toward the warm, inviting rays. Air rushed into the room. It wasn't damp or cold; it did not smell of soot or smoke. Christopher breathed in the wild, sweet air. Could this be what their ancestors had called "fresh air"?

The boy's eyes filled with tears. Grandfather was right. The tiny beam of pure light had been streaming all along from the shaft in the Great Hall, but no one had ever noticed it. No one ever dared to blow out all the lamps in order to see the faint ray of true light.

The people began laughing, admiring their outstretched arms, all glowing rose-red and bathed in light. They dropped their poles and hugged each other, seeing for the first time a sparkle in each other's eyes. No longer were there any dark shadows to be afraid of, for the sunlight showed up everything as it really was.

"Oh, thank you, thank you," Christopher whispered at the sky. "This is the Light we could not see, 'the Light of God that guideth thee.'"

The crowd began cheering, "Oh, happy day. We love the Light we could not see. We love the truth! We want the true Light!"

❧

"I want the light! I want the light!" Chris screamed as he flailed his arms against his bedcovers. He was half-asleep and coming out of the strangest dream he'd ever had. Fully awake now, he sat up in bed. He rubbed his eyes, squinting against the rays of the morning sun streaming into his room.

Chris remembered that he had gone to bed last night with a cloud of darkness filling his heart. He had been holding on to a secret for too many days. It was a simple thing really. No big deal to many, but to Chris, it was a big deal: a forgotten assignment, a half-truth to the teacher, and then a small lie to his folks. No harm done, except for the darkness that had covered him for many days. Chris had been feeling trapped— every day at school and then at home.

He jumped out of bed and walked over to the sliding glass door, letting the warm sun wash over him. Chris opened the door to let in the fresh air of morning. He took a deep breath and then made a simple decision. He was tired of the dark, guilty feelings. What's more, he knew he needed to let go of his lie, just as the cave dwellers had let go of their little lamps.

He would open the door of his heart and tell the truth to his teacher and his parents. He took another deep breath and realized that the fresh air of doing what's right is better than the soot and smoke of guilt, that the light of truth is healthier than living in darkness. As a breeze touched his face, he realized one more thing: truth definitely feels better than a lie.

My Promise To You

God's truth is like sunshine in fresh air. It sweeps away the darkness in our lives, brightens our hearts, and helps us see things as He wants us to see them. I promise always to be God's partner in helping you understand the truth about things. It's better, it's healthier, and, most important, it'll set you free.

_____   _____
SIGNATURE   DATE

HEAVEN'S DOOR

I PROMISE I WILL SHOW YOU THE WAY HOME

. . . Christ is the only foundation.

1 CORINTHIANS 3:11

Stars sparkled like diamonds, a warm breeze whispered through the redwood trees, and from the highest limb where Cirrus and Ariel sat, one could spot a crackling campfire below. It was a heavenly evening as far as they were concerned. And if anyone would know, Cirrus and Ariel would. After all, they were angels.

"What a magnificent night," Cirrus said. He edged farther out on the limb to get a better view of the campsite. "I'm so pleased that the Master sent us to oversee this splendid group of chaps."

Cirrus was talking about Pastor Rob and the sixth grade boys in his youth group. They had pitched their pup tents at the base of the redwood tree. Near the cluster of tents was a picnic table and a couple of sleeping bags spread out by the fire. Ariel tiptoed out on the limb next to Cirrus. He, too, wanted to get a better view, especially since it seemed as though Pastor Rob was about to speak. The angels smiled and winked at one another when he opened his Bible. Nothing pleased them more than to hear a human read the Master's words.

"Okay, guys, listen up," Pastor Rob said as the boys gathered around the fire and tucked their bed rolls under them for a soft seat. One of the kids lingered by a tent. "Hey, Pete," called the pastor, "get the lead out, buddy, and grab a seat over here by the fire. It's time for devotions."

Cirrus balanced himself on the tree limb and pulled an assignment sheet out of his sleeve to scan the names of the campers. "Let's see, whom do we have . . . Justin, Brad, Steven, Travis, Rob—that's the big one—Josh, Noah, Oscar . . . ah, here he is—

43

Pete!" At that point, Cirrus closed his eyes and recited from memory: "Peter Jessup. Father in drug rehab. Mother disappeared. Older brother, gang member. Pete is a bright child. Average student. Few friends. Was placed in foster care with Pastor Rob two months ago and—" Cirrus interrupted his report long enough to watch Pete meander toward the campfire with his hands stuffed in his pockets.

"And?" asked Ariel.

"It's been a rocky two months," Cirrus sighed. Pete elbowed a kid aside and slumped in front of the campfire. Cirrus whispered, "He's in trouble for throwing a knife during recess, breaking into a Coke machine, and stealing change out of the offering plate during Sunday services. But—shhhh—Pastor Rob is about to begin." The two angels slipped from the top of the tree and settled on the picnic table behind the human with his Bible.

After announcements, Pastor Rob began talking about heaven. "It's going to be great," he said. "And just think—we'll have completely brand-new bodies in heaven! Maybe our eyes will have built-in shades. And how about Dolby surround-sound for ears? And wouldn't it be great if our noses came with a choice of scents like Chocolate Factory or Burger Time?"

The boys started giggling. "I think our new bodies in heaven should have noses that are drip-proof!" one of them called out.

"Yeah, and hands with a baseball glove option . . . and feet with Reebok soles . . . and titanium teeth . . . and unlimited aerobic power . . . and a body with adjustable heater and air conditioner!"

All the boys were laughing it up, even Cirrus and Ariel. Everybody was chipping in. Everybody except Pete. "You guys are being stupid," he mumbled.

Pastor Rob heard the comment. He quieted them down. "I'm glad you guys are pumped about heaven, and we've had a good time the last couple of days talking about it. But there's something else about heaven I want you to know. Something that's pretty serious." He kicked a glowing coal with his foot.

He waited a long moment as he stared into the flames. "This fire is diddly-squat compared to the heat turned up in 1 Corinthians 3:11-15. You don't need a merit badge in fire building to get the picture. It says, 'We must be careful how we build because Christ is the only foundation. Whatever we build on that foundation will be tested by fire on the day of judgment. Then everyone will find out if we have used gold, silver, and precious stones, or wood, hay, and straw. We will be rewarded if our building is left standing. But if it is destroyed by the fire, we will lose everything. Yet we ourselves will be saved, like someone escaping from flames.'"

Cirrus and Ariel leaned forward to see the boys better. As angels, they always wanted to know how humans would respond to the Word of God. Especially human boys. And even more especially, someone like Pete.

"I thought heaven was supposed to be a nice place," Pete sneered. The angels shot each other a knowing smile. They knew the Master had been working on Pete the past couple of months. Things happening in his life . . . things fitting together just so . . . and a powerful push on his heart straight from the throne of heaven. All the attention was beginning to pay off: Pete was showing an interest in the Bible, even if it was to argue with it.

"It *is* a neat place," piped up one of the others.

"That's right," Pastor Rob agreed. "And this judgment has nothing to do with getting into heaven. That's signed, sealed, and delivered once you ask Jesus to be your Savior and mean it. No, this judgment is different. It says if you do dumb things with your life, you're sending ahead to heaven a bunch of wood, hay, and straw. For instance, if your whole life revolves around roller-blading, GameBoy, and finding new ways to cheat on tests then, hey, that's highly flammable stuff."

The boys were hugging their knees and listening. Especially Pete. The words struck home. Pastor Rob continued, "But every time you obey your mom, walk away from a fight, pray for others, or sing Scripture choruses at church and *mean* it, then you are sending ahead to heaven beams made of gold and bricks of silver, and nuts and bolts made from precious stones. You're building up for the greatest joy ever. It's treasure that will last you for eternity."

The kids were fascinated. They started asking Pastor Rob all sorts of questions. Good questions about the kinds of things that last and don't last, including good choices and bad ones. Cirrus and Ariel slapped each other on the back. They began jotting notes about each boy on the assignment list. They couldn't help but notice, though, that Pete was looking the other way and staring into the dark forest.

Cirrus and Ariel turned their attention to Pastor Rob. It was obvious he loved these boys. And it was clear he was concerned for their eternal life. "He is doing a pretty good job of preaching, too," Ariel said with a smile.

That's when it happened. Out of the blue, out of nowhere, as though bursting through a thin layer of cellophane, a big golden 2 x 4 beam suddenly appeared before the angels' eyes. "Whoa!" they exclaimed. "Would you look at *this!*" Cirrus and Ariel shoved their lists up their sleeves just in time to free up their hands to catch the golden beam. It had Pastor Rob's name on it. "Now *this* is something to take back home to heaven tonight," Cirrus said as he held the large golden 2 x 4.

The campfire discussion about heaven lasted long after the burning logs died down. Later that night, the boys crawled into their sleeping bags feeling tired and happy. This was no surprise to the angels as they looked on from their perch on the picnic table. They saw it happen to humans all the time when talk turned to heaven. Cirrus and Ariel glanced over their shoulders. The picnic table was piled high with gold, silver, and precious stones to be carried back to heaven that night.

Cirrus was about to take a break and head back to heaven (with gold and silver in tow) when Ariel grabbed his arm. Trouble was afoot over by one of the tents. "Pete? Pete?" Pastor Rob called out quietly to keep from waking the others. The angels hopped down from the table and scurried ahead of Pastor Rob to search for the boy.

Ariel moved behind the far tent and then stopped. There, only five feet away, hunched Pete with a pack of matches. The boy struck a match, lit a small pile of dry leaves, and stepped back. A thin curl of smoke appeared, and then with a whooshing sound, the fire suddenly exploded. Flames leaped high into the air, licking the back of the tent. Pete jumped back. He wanted to stop it, but he froze with fright.

Cirrus ran up behind Ariel. "Oh, no!" he gasped. The two angels quickly decided to break through the thin cellophane-like barrier separating their world from the humans' world. They waved their big wings to blow the smoke Pastor Rob's way. It worked! Within seconds, he was on the scene.

"Pete! What are you doing?" Pastor Rob grabbed a sleeping bag and threw it over the fire. After he stomped out the last of the burning leaves, he turned to Pete who had backed up against a tree. The boy shivered. He covered his face, expecting the usual slap his older brother would have given him—or the stinging words. Or maybe Pastor Rob would just walk away like his dad had done. Pete peeked out from under his elbow, wondering why the man wasn't yelling.

In the next instant, Pastor Rob's arms tightly hugged the little boy. "Oh, Pete, you're safe! You're okay! You're not hurt!" Pete couldn't believe it. For the first time in two months, he dared to wrap his arms around his foster dad. Tears of fright gave way to sobs of relief and joy.

They weren't the only ones crying. Cirrus and Ariel were holding on to each other and crying, too. Finally Cirrus huffed, "You're getting me all wet!" They started laughing and looked to see that the man and the little boy were smiling, too.

Pastor Rob cupped Pete's wet face in his hands. "Can you just tell me one thing?" he asked gently. "Why did you set those leaves on fire?"

Pete looked down and shuffled his feet in what remained of the leaves. "I don't know. . . . I guess I wanted to see how hay and straw burns . . . since everything I do is just a bunch of straw. I don't belong there," he said, gesturing toward the sky, "and I don't belong here. I don't even belong to you."

"Oh, son, you're mistaken," Pastor Rob said softly.

"Son?" Pete asked, wiping a tear from his eye.

Pastor Rob folded his arms around the boy and squeezed him against his chest.

"Yes, Pete," he whispered, "we have a long, long time to discover all that that word means. You belong here with us. With me. And speaking of being a son," he said, as he held Pete at arm's length, "God wants to welcome you as His child, too."

Moments later, Ariel and Cirrus stood breathless as they watched Pastor Rob and Pete pray. Next to hearing a human read the Bible and preach the Gospel, the best thing was to hear a person pray to Jesus, their Master, for the first time. And that's exactly what Pete did! It meant even more to the angels when they heard the boy say, "I'm sorry. . . . I was wrong." It showed them Pete meant it from the heart.

Ariel gave Cirrus a high five as they walked back to the picnic table. They weren't prepared, however, for the huge surprise that awaited them. There was no table! It was hidden underneath humongous blocks of gold, each block shaped to fit with the others. Ariel, full of the joy that only heaven's angels feel when a brand-new Christian is born, jumped up on top of the large blocks.

"This is awesome!" Cirrus said, as he walked up to one of the stones and ran his hands over the smooth surface. "And look, Ariel, look at this."

Ariel kneeled down. What he saw was enough to make him fold his wings and bow his head. Cirrus, too. For each stone was engraved with the name of the Master. From here on out, the angels knew that Pete had a foundation for his life. The only foundation. Jesus.

My Promise To You

Whenever I can point you to Jesus, I am pointing you to the way home, because to think about heaven is to think about Him. I promise to help you keep building things that last in your life, whether it's the gold of obedience, the silver of good thoughts, or the precious stones of loving others. One more thing: Is Jesus the foundation in your life?
If so, great. . . . Let's get building. If not, then how about you and me praying right now like Pastor Rob and Pete?

_____   _____
SIGNATURE   DATE

Other books in the series:

Tell Me the Story
BY MAX LUCADO WITH RON DiCIANNI

Tell Me the Secrets
BY MAX LUCADO WITH RON DiCIANNI